DES DILLON is an internationally [acclaimed] writer. He was born in Coatbri[dge and studied] Literature at Strathclyde University before becoming a teacher. He was Writer-in-Residence at Castlemilk from 1998–2000. He is a poet, short story writer, novelist, dramatist, broadcaster, screen writer, and scriptwriter for TV, stage and radio. His books have been published in the USA, India, Russia, Sweden, in Catalan, French and Spanish. His novel *Me and Ma Gal* was shortlisted for the Saltire Society Scottish First Book of the Year Award and won the World Book Day 'We Are What We Read' poll for the novel that best describes Scotland today. His poetry has been anthologised internationally. His latest award was The Lion and Unicorn prize for the best of Irish and British Literature in the Russian Language (2007). Des lives in Galloway with his wife and two dogs.

Also by Des Dillon:

Fiction
Me and Ma Gal (1995)
The Big Empty: A Collection of Short Stories (1996)
Duck (1998)
Itchycooblue (1999)
Return of the Busby Babes (2000)
Six Black Candles (2002)
The Blue Hen (2004)
The Glasgow Dragon (2004)
They Scream When You Kill Them (2006)
Monks (2007)
My Epileptic Lurcher (2008)

Poetry
Picking Brambles (2003)

Singin I'm No A Billy He's A Tim

DES DILLON

Luath Press Limited
EDINBURGH
www.luath.co.uk

First published 2005
This edition 2008

ISBN (10): 1-906307-46-6
ISBN (13): 978-1-906307-46-2

Des Dillon has asserted his rights
under the Copyright, Designs and Patents Act 1988
to be identified as the author of this work.

The paper used in this book is recyclable. It is made from
low-chlorine pulps produced in a low-energy, low-emission
manner from renewable forests.

The publisher acknowledges subsidy from
Scottish Arts Council
towards the publication of this volume.

Printed in the UK by CPI Bookmarque, Croydon CR0 4TD

Typeset in Frutiger and Sabon

© Des Dillon, 2005

*This book is dedicated to Posh, Furious, DE5 and Pindy.
Cos without these cunts the play would never have happened.*

Extract from 'Caledonia' reproduced by kind permission of
Dougie MacLean. Music & lyrics by Dougie MacLean.
Published by Limetree Arts and Music. This song is included
on the following Dougie MacLean CDs available from Dunkeld
Records: *Craigie Dhu* (1983), *Live – From the Ends of the
Earth* (2000) and *With Strings* (2003).

Force adversaries to talk and they will find a peace.

This book is about bigotry and ethnic identity.
What happens when, on the day of the Old Firm match, you lock a Celtic and a Rangers fan in a cell together?
Fireworks. And a weird kind of unity.

Shortly after the tsunami disaster a Sri Lankan minister was seen talking to a Tamil Tiger leader. They had never spoken before. They seemed to get on well. Adversity had thrown them together and forced them to talk, and in responding to the needs of others they found common ground; a shared humanity; a starting point.

This book is an allegory for the Irish Peace Process and peace processes all over the world.

1

There is a cell with a hatch looking out onto a short corridor. Along a short corridor is the turnkey's office. Upstage is a T junction to a cell block corridor we don't see, and a security door into the courthouse.

Inside the cell: a stainless steel toilet; a concrete bunk with a thin pvc mattress; a surveillance camera; a hatch which the inmates can use to look out into the corridor; a toilet; a roll of toilet paper. In the office: a telly; a CCTV screen; a phone; a chair and a table.

In the dark cell, Harry, a 50-something turnkey, holds his mobile phone in the air looking for a signal. A buzzer goes and Harry leaves through a door, switching the cell lights on as he goes.

Harry (*off*) Come on. Quiet lads. (*they quieten*) Once your fines're paid you're getting out. Right you, back from the door. (*Harry appears in the corridor with Tim, 25, in a Celtic top. Tim reacts*) Step this way madam.

Tim Goanny stop squeezin ma arm. That's sore.

Harry walks Tim to the cell.

Harry Shoes. (*Tim takes off his green and white training shoes*) Belt.

Tim I've no belt.

Harry Is there a drawstring in them?

Tim shows Harry his trakkies.

Tim Elasticated – look – (*Tim pulls them and lets them twang back*) I'd hang myself a thousand times if I done it wi them. Boing boing!

Harry smiles and opens the door. Pushes Tim gently in.

Harry Ring the bell for room service. Let's hope your wife can raise the other – how much is it?

Tim Hunner an sixty.

Harry   Och! The game's just starting, you could be there for half time.

Door slams. Key turns. Harry goes back to his office. Tim sighs. Looks round the cell.

Tim   Fuckin bummer. (*Tim boots the door*) Shit – shit – fuckin shit!

Harry   (*from office*) Hey hey hey! Calm down son.

Tim slumps onto the bed and sighs, lies down and starts humming an Irish song. The humming morphs into singing.

Tim   Where are the lads,
Who stood with me,
When history was made...
(*He repeats made over and over listening to the echo*) Made... made... made...

2

Harry lifts the phone and listens to the dialling tone. He puts it down and RING! RING! He jolts back with fright as the phone goes. Harry picks it up a bit too hastily almost letting it drop. Tim stands up and listens intently at the hatch.

Harry   Hello. Is he alright? (*It's not who he thought it was*) Right. No I thought you were someone else there. (*reaches for a pen*) Give me the names. (*Harry writes down a load of names. He takes out his keys. Harry shouts into the cell block as he walks into it. Tim still listens at his door*) Buchanan. Riley. Ferguson. Gallagher. (*Doors open and people get out*) Morning ladies – paid in full. You're free to go. Collect your possessions upstairs.

Diminishing footsteps and slam of the big courthouse door. When Tim hears Harry's footsteps coming back he rattles on the door.

Tim   Hey – turnkey. Turnkey! Ye out there? (*Harry is outside Tim's cell wondering whether or not to respond. Tim looks this way and that through the hatch*) Boss!? Hello!? Is there anybody there?

Silence a beat, then:

Harry   (*getting a fright*) My name's not boss and it's not turnkey.

Tim   Sorry, boss. I mean sorry…

Harry   Harry – my name's Harry.

Tim   Harry.

Harry   What is it?

Tim   Was ma name not on that list?

Harry   No. It wasn't.

Tim   Shit. I need to get out of here!

Harry   Soon as it's paid you're off!

Tim   It's as good as paid.

Harry   You'll make the second half then.

Tim   Can ye not jist let me out? I'll pay it,
        I promise!

Harry   You're in here for promising!

Tim thinks a beat, then:

Tim   Well, have you got a telly in yer wee office
        then?

Harry   I don't see as that's any of your business.

Tim   Ye have!

Harry   How do you know?

Tim   I can see it.

Harry   Aye, and?

Tim   And – any chance of turnin it round so as
        I can see the game?

Harry   It may have escaped your notice – but
        you're in jail.

Tim   Aw come on Harry.

Harry   Surely you're not that addicted to football.

Tim   It's not jist the football.

Harry   What is it then?

Tim   Don't gimmi that – you fine well know what it is!

Harry   Do I?

They stare at each other a beat.

Tim   There's more to football than football Harry!

Harry looks at Tim and because he knows this is true he changes the subject.

Harry   I'm sure your wife'll be along with the money soon – you're the only one left in.

Tim   There's no chance of her turnin up before the end of the game, ma wife.

Harry   How's that? She ran away with Bobo Balde?

Tim   Aw ha ha! I sent her away to stick every last curdy on Celtic to win so I did. To get me out.

Harry   Ri—ght! Good one. I see.

Tim   So can ye turn it round so as I can see the game?

Harry   There's a rule book son.

Tim   Aw come on Harry, don't be rotten man!

> Jist the sound then. So as I can hear it at least. (*Harry walks away. Tim shouts*) I've got to see the game!

Harry That's a good one right enough – I've seen it all now. Your wife gambling to get your liberty.

Tim (*shouts*) It's not a gamble Harry. It's the Celtic!

Harry I've got cells to clean.

Tim (*shouts*) Goanny put the light out in this cell then? At least I can get a kip.

Harry lifts the bucket and leaves, putting the lights out as he goes.

3

We can barely see Tim in the dimmed light. He starts singing low and falls away into a snoring sleep.

Tim   For it's a grand old team to play for –
sure it's a grand old team to know –
for if – you know – the history –
it's enough to make your heart grow
oh oh we don't care what the animals say –
what the hell do we care –
for we only know
that there's going to be a show
and the Glasgow Celtic will be there…

By now Tim is snoring loudly. The official buzzer goes. We hear a heavy prison door swing open.

Harry   (*eventually appearing*) Step this way, madam.

Harry brings in Billy, 25, Rangers fan. Billy is angry.

Billy   Judge is a fuckin maniac! Been snortin too much coke.

Harry   Calm down son.

Billy   Sticks me doon here – tells ma wife to go'n raise the money.

Harry   You're a latecomer.

Billy   I'm the last wan.

Harry   Are you? Good! Off to the game?

Billy   Aye – how'd ye know that? (*Harry tugs his Rangers top*) Och – I forgoat I had this oan wi gettin lifted an that.

They arrive outside Tim's cell.

Harry   Shoes. (*Billy takes off his red white and blue shoes Harry sits them beside Tim's green and white ones*) Belt.

Billy   No got wan! (*Harry puts the key in the lock and turns it. The door opens. Billy goes in. Harry closes the door*) Hey! It's pitch black in here.

Harry   (*walking away*) I'll switch the light back on. When I'm cleaning the cells.

Harry leaves. Billy hears the snoring. He peers as he moves through the darkness. He hits the toilet. Tim jerks awake.

Billy   Who's that!

Tim   (*waking*) Who's that?

Billy   Fuckin fines.

Tim   I'm the same. Gettin ready for the game. Bastards crashed in an lifted me.

Billy   I was eatin ma breakfast. Ham 'n eggs an aw. Bunch of cunts.

Tim   Can they not catch drug dealers or somethin? Here (*slaps the bench*) huv a seat.

Tim beats on he bench till Billy stumbles over and sits down.

Billy   Wife never had the money.

Tim   Neither did mine.

An awkward beat, then they peer at each other. Harry remembers the light. The light clicks on. In shock, they get up and stumble back from each other. Tim stares at Billy with his mouth hanging open.

Tim   Ye're kiddin!

Billy   Aw whit the fuck is this?

Tim crashes to the hatch.

Tim   (*to Harry*) Ye're fuckin kiddin!

Billy sticks his head through, shouting.

Billy   Hey – is this some kinda sick joke? Ye've stuck me in here wi this Fenian bastard. (*BANG! Tim boots Billy up the arse*) Agh! Ya fuckin bastard!

They grab each other by the hair and spin round the cell.

Tim   Let go.

Billy   You let go first.

Tim   No, you let go.

Billy   I'm not lettin go!

Harry comes rushing back and into the cell.

Tim   Argh! Ma head!

Harry   Right come on!

Harry pushes them to opposite corners.

Tim   That fuckin door hut me on the head there.

Harry   Right what's the score?

Tim   Is ma head bleedin?

Billy   He attacked me.

Tim   I attacked you? It was that cunt that attacked me! Look!

Tim shows Harry his head.

Billy   Ye said it was the door that done that.

Tim   (*to Harry*) It was him.

Billy   Ye jist sayed it was the door!!

Harry   What ye talking about. That door opens outwards. (*avuncular*) Let me see.

Harry inspects Tim's head.

Billy   Watch out for nits!

Harry   Nothing.

Tim   Nothing? It's killin me. It's like that – throb throb.

Tim feels his head and searches his fingers for blood.

Harry   (*firm now*) Now what's going on?

Billy   He booted me up the arse.

Harry turns to Tim.

Harry   Did you boot him up the arse?

Tim   Aye! (*to Billy*) What ye goin to do? Sue me?

Billy   Aye – for half your fuckin Giro!

Tim   I'll half my fuckin Giro ye!

Harry   What did you boot him up the arse for?

Tim   Comes in dressed like the Union Jack – calls me a Fenian bastard and I'm supposed to take it?

Billy   I'm no sharin a cell wi him.

Tim   Fuckin ditto Bluto.

Billy   I'll fuckin Bluto ye!

Harry   (*shouts*) Right! (*Billy and Tim stop. Harry points to the top of the cell*) See that. (*They both swing and are shocked to see a camera*) Everything you do is recorded. I could get the cops right now and have you both done with assault. Then you'd be here all weekend. Up in front of MacIlraith on

Monday morning. Christ knows how he'll take that! (*Billy and Tim stare at each other*) Is that what you want? Cos I can arrange it. (*Billy shakes his head; then to Tim*) Well?

Tim   No.

Harry   Good. I've got work to do. There's more to life than all this pish.

Harry tugs at both their football tops. Lets them go with a sharp snap and leaves, then goes to his office and picks up his knitting.

Tim   Fuckin nightmare.

Tim guards the bench as both men strut their macho stuff about the cell.

4

Tim claims the bench and Billy eventually lies on the floor. Then – there's the sound of knitting needles. Billy homes in on it – trying to identify the noise.

Billy (*to himself*) What is that? (*the sound of knitting needles continues*) What the fuck is that?

Tim (*to himself*) Sounds like fuckin knittin needles. (*Tim gets up and goes to the hatch*) It is, it is knittin needles. (*Tim gets up on bench for a look*) He's sittin there like that – knit one purl one. (*Billy looks*) Stops him gettin bored I suppose. (*to Billy*) I wish I'd a pair of knittin needles the now.

Billy What would ye knit – a conspiracy!!?? (*Billy falls about laughing at his own joke*) A conspiracy!

Tim   No. I'd stick them in your fuckin head.

But Billy still laughs.

Billy   A conspiracy. That was a belter.

Tim   Listen to him – laughin at his own patter!

The phone rings, interrupting Billy's sniggering. Harry snatches the phone up. Tim makes for the hatch. For a beat Billy thinks Tim is on the attack.

Billy   What's your game?

Tim   I like listenin to phone calls – right.

As Tim listens, Billy takes his trakkie top off and uses it as a pillow.

Harry   Aye. It's me. Okay okay – calm down.

Tim   He's tryin to calm somebody down.

Harry   I am calm. So what did they say? They must've said something?

Tim   Somethin's wrong.

Harry   Och I suppose they know what they're doing right enough. Look – good luck hen. I'm on the end of the phone. (*afterthought*) Have ye got my mobile number an all? Has Bobby got it?

Tim   Sounds like he's waitin on news.

Harry   Aw have ye? How's Bobby? No, he wouldn't send me a message. He's not even got my mobile. Did ye?

Tim   Somebody called Bobby.

Harry   Any news at all – anything – just phone me. Bye. Bye.

Tim   Interesting. (*Harry lifts his mobile and heads towards the cell. Tim jumps*) Fuck – he's comin!

But Harry stops, looking for an excuse to go in. He lifts two cans of coke. Harry comes in.

Harry   You two calmed down yet?

Billy   Aye.

Tim   Mm mm.

Harry   Couple of cans of coke that were in the office. Keep you cool.

Harry just stands there and Billy and Tim are confused at that.

Billy   (*confused*) Cheers.

Tim   (*confused*) Cheers.

Harry gives them to Billy. Billy holds one out to Tim and retracts it a couple of times before Tim grabs it.

Tim Fuckin geez it.

Billy and Tim open the cans. Harry fiddles with his mobile phone. Harry keeps looking at the phone. It's excruciating silence and looks. (cos Harry wants to try for a signal on his phone) Then, eventually:

Billy I'm goanny be in for a month at least.

Harry (*Jumping on that*) What's that son?

Billy I owe a grand. Where's my wife goanny get that?

Harry That's a big fine.

Billy Ringin a couple of oul cars.

Tim Oul cars!

Billy Is there a fuckin echo in here?

Harry Hey! (*Billy backs down*) Why don't you do what Tim done?

Billy (*snorting*) Tim!

Tim What ye laughin at?

Billy   That his name? Fuckin Tim?

Tim   What's funny about that?

Billy   Nothing. First Tim I've met called Tim. That's all. Fuckin Tim man!

Tim   What's your name like? Patrick Aloysius? (*beat as Billy realises he's been caught out*) Well? What is your fuckin name anyway?

Billy   (*turning his back to the audience and revealing Billy on his back*) Fuckin Billy.

Laughter. Harry is amused.

Tim   (*laughing*) Billy. Ya wank. Billy!

Harry   See yees later, lads.

Harry tries to leave.

Billy   Turnkey!

Tim   Harry!

Billy   What?

Tim   He likes to get called Harry.

Billy   Harry! (*Billy invades Harry's space*) What was it ye were sayin aboot what he done?

Harry   Ask him.

Billy   Well I'm no talkin to him, am I? (*Tim mouths I'm no talking to him*) I'm askin you.

Harry   (*relenting*) Got his wife to put money on Celtic to win.

Billy   Donno know what ye mean.

Harry   Celtic win. His wife pays his fine. He's out!

Billy gets it. Tim lies on the bed, exuding pride.

Tim   See – I'm not as daft as you look, ya pie muncher.

Billy   But how do I get a bet oan fae here?
Harry shrugs.

Tim   Oh! There's a Ladbrokes in the next cell!

Billy looks at Harry's phone – looks at Harry.

Harry   Oh I don't know.

Billy   Come oan! Wan call!

Harry   If anyone found out – it would be my job.

Billy   Ye can say ye dropped it. In here when we were fightin. (*Harry's thinking about it*) Please Harry. I wullnae say nothin. It would really mean a lot to me.

Harry Ach!

Billy (*Billy takes the phone from Harry*) Cheers mate.

Billy goes to the corner looking for a signal.

Harry You can sometimes get a signal standing on top of the bunk.

Billy pushes Tim aside.

Tim Get aff me. (*Tim complains to Harry*) D'you see that there? Tried to stand on me. That's assault that, so it is.

Harry I'll sit here then. Keep yous apart. (*to Billy*) Can you check if there's any messages on that son – if you get a signal. Just in case.

Billy Signal! (*Harry is eager*) Nothin. No messages. (*Harry's face falls*) It's ringin. Hello?

Tim (*sings*) Hello – Hello – We are the Billy boys…

Harry dunts Tim.

Billy Hello darlin, it's me. Aye – I'm fine. Honest. There's people listenin. There's people

listenin, I said. Right – I swear oan King
Billy's horse. (*Tim nudges Harry trying to
get him to listen*) I sayed it. (*Tim kicks Harry
to listen*) I swear oan King Billy's horse that
I'm okay. They've locked me up wi a Celtic
fan. They did. Honest. Fuck! Hey Tim. (*to
wife*) No, that is his name, honest. (*to Tim*)
You've to say hello.

Tim   (*sings*) Hello – Hello – I am a Celtic fan...

Billy   I know he is a wank... No I canny. Cos this
is where they put me. (*confirming with
Harry*) They're gettin cleaned. Listen. Is
there still five hunner in the Halifax?
Here's what I want ye to dae. Go doon
the bookies. Shove it oan Rangers to win.
When the game's finished, go'n collect the
money an come pay ma fine. Me too.
Honest. There's people listenin. (*he sighs*)
Love you too.

Tim   (*mouthing*) Love you too.

Billy   (*eyeing Tim*) See ye efter doll. (*Billy hangs
up, sinks Tim with a look, and gives the
phone back to Harry*) Cheers for that, Harry.

Harry   Cheers for what?

Billy   (*Billy stands and goes to the door*) Harry, ye
haven't got a radio in that wee office of
yours have ye?

Tim   He's got a telly.

Billy   A telly – ya fuckin dancer!

Harry   No can do, lads. I've already told him.

They pile the pressure on Harry.

Tim   Harry!

Billy   Harry mate!

Tim   Come on!

Harry   I said no.

Billy   So we've just to sit in here wonderin if we're getting out or no?

Harry   I'll keep you up to date.

Tim   Aw thanks – thanks a fuckin million.

Billy   At least turn it oan an keep yer office door open a bit.

Tim   Come on Harry – we're the only cunts in here.

Billy   Ye can turn it off if anybody comes.

Tim   Come on Harry! They've got to buzz down for ye!

Harry   (*bursting away from them*) Right, right, right! But if anyone comes in – it's off!

Billy   Good man.

Tim   Cheers Harry.

Harry walks away. Billy goes to the hatch in anticipation. Harry opens his office door but doesn't close it. He switches on the telly. We can hear the hazy sound of the match but can't make it out.

Billy   Canny hear a fuckin thing.

Tim   Let me try. (*Tim listens with all his might*) Nothin. Jist the crowd.

Billy pulls Tim away and shouts out.

Billy   Harry!

Tim   Harry!!

Billy   Here he comes.

Harry comes up to the hatch.

Harry   What is it now?

Billy   What's the score?

Harry   Nothing each. Are you not listening?

Billy   Canny hear it.

Harry   I've opened the door.

Tim   We canny hear it but!

Harry   I've opened the door.

Billy   Come oan Harry, geez a break.

Tim   Our freedom's gambled on this game an we can't even hear it.

Billy   Keeps echoin roon the place.

Harry   I didn't design the buildings, son.

Billy   Turn it up then.

Harry   I canny.

Tim   Jist a tad!

Harry   I canny.

Billy   Everybody else is away.

Harry   I canny.

Tim   How can ye not?

Harry   Cos it's fucked – that's as loud as it goes!

Tim   Oh!

Harry shrugs and walks away and takes up his knitting.

Billy   What a fuckin day.

Tim   Nightmare.

Billy   He doesn't look like a knitter does he?

Tim   What does a knitter look like?

Harry sighs, gets up, takes a chair out into the hall. He comes back and takes the telly out. Lines it up with the cell.

Tim   Hey – is that not getting louder?

Billy   Aye. Fuckin is.

Tim   Is that no music to yer fuckin ears man?

Billy goes to the hatch.

Billy   Aw – Harry – you are a gentleman. A true gentleman.

Harry smiles to himself.

Tim   What is it?

Billy pulls his head back in and grins at Tim.

Billy   Ye want to see what he's done.
Billy, butler style, guides Tim to the hatch. Billy savours his reaction.

Tim   We're goanny see the game. We're goanny see the game!

They hug like two players after a crucial goal has been scored. But when they realise what they're doing they break free and cover. Awkward pause, then:

5

Billy goes to the hatch.

Billy   Right em – chances each.

Tim   Who says?

Billy   I says.

Tim   How d'you get to say?

Billy   Tell iz a fairer way then?

Tim can't think of a fairer way.

Billy   Shh! Aw Ferguson ya dick!!

After a few beats, Tim starts singing.

Tim   By lonely prison walls...
   I heard a young girl callin,

Michael they have taken you away...
(*continues. Harry leaves*)

Billy I wish you lot would shut up wi that shite.

Tim It's my heritage.

Billy Yer heritage!

Tim There's nothin wrong wi rememberin yer heritage.

Billy I bet ye've never even been in Ireland. (*Beat as Tim squirms*) Have ye?

Tim I'm not tellin you where I've been an where I've not.

A beat, then:

Billy Ye've never been have ye? (*Tim ignores him*) Answer me then.

Tim So! What if I haven't?

Billy Yees're aw the same – rattlin oan aboot a place ye've never been. If I had my way I'd send yees aw back to fuckin tattie land.

Tim Oh not that oul wan.

Billy If ye're Irish, ye should live in fuckin Ireland.

Tim   What about the Italians an the Pakis an the Indians an the Chinkees.

Billy   Chinkees?

Tim   Aye – what ye not sendin them back to China for. Eh? In case they chop ye up – choppy choppy choppy – big fuckin cleaver – choppy choppy Proddy curry. Won hun soup.

Billy   Stop changin the subject. We were talkin about you never havin been to Ireland.

Tim   A lot of Pakis've never been to Pakistan!

Billy   That's halfway roon the world. Not jist over there!

Tim   We've been here before any of them! So if there's anybody ye should be sendin home it should be them.

Billy   Let me guess – yer family came ower here in the tattie famine.

Tim   Aye. When yours were still hidin under a rock in Airdrie.

Billy   (*sudden pique*) Ma heritage goes straight as a die to Ulster.

Tim   Aw – have you been there? (*No answer*) Have ye?

Billy   Aye!

Tim   Have ye fuck.

Billy   Aye – I have!

Tim   When?

Billy   Fuckin years ago, right.

Tim   Up Shankhill Road wi a big drum and a tray fulla pies. Wanny they daft wee hat hings. What they called – doughball hats?

Billy   Not dougball hats. Bowler hats. Like people wear when they're goin to their *work*!

Tim   Right you, out the way. It's my turn.

Tim watches the game ad-libbing comments. Billy footers about with the toilet roll. He gets an idea. He takes a long length off and ties it into a loop. He drapes it over his shoulder.

Billy   Hey!? (*Tim turns – Billy sings and marches round the cell – twirls a stick and throws it in the air*) It is old and it is beautiful, and its colours they are fine…

Tim eventually laughs at that.

Billy   That's ma wee sash man!

When the laughter dies away enough Tim offers this:

Tim   Rangers wasn't always a Proddy team ye know.

Billy   What ye fuckin talkin aboot?

Tim   It was Harland and Wolfe men that came to the shipyards here. They turned Rangers into an Orange team. Your *ancestors*. Your fuckin *heritage*!

Billy   You believe what ye want to believe an I'll believe the truth.

Tim   Don't worry, I will.

Billy   Good.

Tim   Fine!

A beat, then:

Billy   Right – here's a question for ye. Are you Irish or Scottish?

Tim   Irish.

Billy   That'll be how ye've got a Donegal accent.

Tim   My accent's Scottish but my culture's Irish.

Billy   Ooh! Culture. Big fuckin fancy words. Right. Who would ye support if Scotland were playin Ireland?

Tim   Scotland.

Billy   I though ye were Irish?

Tim   Ma culture's Irish – I sayed.

Billy   But ye sayed ye're not Scottish.

Tim   No I never.

Billy   Aye ye did – I sayed are ye Scottish or Irish an you clearly fuckin sayed Irish!

Tim   Ah! But I never sayed I wasn't Scottish either, did I?

Billy   Ye never answered ma question.

Tim   What question?

Billy   Wan minute ye're Irish next hing ye're supportin Scotland. Does that no strike ye as a bit odd?

Tim   No – it's very simple – I'm an Irish Scot.

Billy   An Irish Scot. Oh fuck – I've heard it aw noo.

An Irish Scot. (*choking laughter*) An Irish Scot!

Tim What?

Billy Born in Coatbridge – never even smelt Ireland – an he's an Irish Scot.

Tim See – that's the reaction ye get every time ye say that.

Billy No fuckin wonder.

Tim What's up wi bein an Irish Scot?

Billy Nothin – I'm a tangerine banana.

Tim No – ye're an Orange bastard. (*Billy suppresses his anger and gives Tim the got-you look*) I'm talkin about me bein Irish and ma culture an you keep bringin it back to bigotry.

Billy How long've ye been here?

Tim Four generations.

Billy Well then! Surely ye're fuckin Scottish noo.

Tim What is Scottish Billy? (*Billy's caught off guard*) Eh? Tell me what bein Scottish is?

Billy (*struggling*) Fuckin... like...

Tim   (*taunting*) Tell me.

Billy   Right, haud on – I'm thinkin.

Tim   (*pressuring*) Come on.

Billy   Eh...

Tim   Come on! (*Tim snap snap snaps his fingers in Billy's face*) Answer me Billy answer – answer – answer.

Billy   (*snap answer*) Like me! You've goat to be like me.

Tim   Like you? That would make me an Orangeman – so how the fuck's that Scottish? (*Billy says nothing*) That's right. You stay shut up cos you don't represent Scotland any more than fuckin Oor Wullie does.

Billy   You shouldn't be allowed a fuckin opinion anyway. (*anger*) We took yees in! An how do yees repay us. By blowing us up!

Tim   I never blew anybody up.

Billy   No? Manchester. Birmingham. Warrington. Fuckin London!

Tim   It wasn't fuckin me but, was it!

Billy   No but I bet ye didn't condemn it either did ye? Did ye? (*beat on Tim*) No – none of yees did. Not even your priests. (*Tim can't speak*) (*Tim goes to speak. Billy bulldozes him*) Don't fuckin pull all that culture shite out on me again.

Tim   Well what should we do about it Billy? Eh come on tell me?

Billy   Test them.

Tim   Test them?

Billy   Aye. Fuckin test them.

A look of incredulity from Tim, then:

Tim   What, on fuckin arithmetic?

Billy   No – no fuckin arithmetic. Football. The ones that support Scotland can stay. But them that support Ireland can get to fuck back to Ireland.

Tim   Good idea. Fling the Indians out for supportin their cricket team, or the Pakis – or the Italians— they've got the greatest football team in the world! D'you want them to just ignore that?

Billy   (*rage*) We fuckin took yees in!

Tim	Aye, yees took us in alright. Refused us work then called us lazy. Starved us and called us thieves.

Billy	(*chanting*) Paranoia! Paranoia!

Tim	Paranoia is it? Funny how people can be Italian Americans, Irish Americans, African Americans, but soon as I say I'm an Irish Scot, sure as fuck, cunts like you are on me like a pack of hounds. How's that, son? Eh? Eh?

Billy	Could it be that ye're talkin through a hole in yer arse?

Tim	You know fine well what it is!

Billy	Do I?

Tim	Aye.

Billy	Do I?

Tim	Aye ye fuckin do! All yous cunts know.

Billy	Enlighten me.

Tim	En–ligh–ten – Whoo! who's usin the big words now?

Billy	That's what comes from a (*slight pause*) proper education.

Tim   Oh. What else did they teach ye in that Proddy school? Ethnic cleansin?

A beat, then:

Billy   No. Big words – like – Pa-ra-noi-a!

Tim   Paranoia!? There's anti Catholic shite goin on everywhere.

Billy   Where?

Tim   All round about.

Billy   Gimmi an example then.

Tim   I will give ye an example, right!

Billy   Go well.

Tim   Right, gee me a fuckin minute an I will.

Billy   Come oan – come oan – hurry up (*Billy snaps his fingers in Tim's face now*) What's up? No like it? Can give it but can't take it.

Tim   I can't think when you're yap yap yappin in ma face, can I?

Billy   Guinness pressure's sky high Michael.

Tim   (*finding something at last*) When the Pope died!

Billy   (*abruptly silent*) What?

Tim   When the fuckin Pope died – the SFA
         avoided orderin a minute's silence till it was
         too late.

Billy   They had one at the Hearts–Celtic game.

Tim   Thank you! Aye and what happened there?
         Eh. Can't hear ye Billy! Fuckin Hearts fans
         ruined it! Come on Billy, what did they do?
         (*continues pressing*)

But Billy doesn't want to hear it – nor answer – so he sings:

Billy   I'm Pope eye the shamrock man,
         I'm the world's most paranoid man,
         I'm dyin wi rabies
         From chewin Orange babies
         I'm Pope eye the shamrock man.
         Boom Boom!
         (*Billy stops – a nuclear fusion of
         anger – takes up his position at the hatch*)
         Come oan the Gers!!!! Novo! OOH! Nearly
         fucked yees there. Here have another
         tattie!

Tim   How can I? You et them all. (*As Billy
         watches the game Tim's huff is doing
         overtime looking for retaliation*) Here's a
         question for ye then.

Billy   Fire away but don't expect me to take ma eyes off this – whoof – game.

Tim   Are you Scottish?

Billy   British – an fuckin proud of it, mate.

Tim   Now who's talkin through a hole in their arse? *You* were born in Scotland – *you've* got a Scottish accent.

Billy   (*points to arm*) See that Union Jack. I'm British.

Tim   All right. If Scotland were playin England, who would ye support?

Billy thinks about that for a moment, then:

Billy   Scotland.

Tim   Bang! Case closed!

Billy   What ye oan aboot – bang case closed!? I can still be British an support Scotland!

Tim   Good, well – I can be Scottish an support Ireland.

Billy   Ye said ye supported Scotland.

Tim   Aw fuck – it's an example.

Billy   Aye, you are a fuckin example!

Tim   Oh fuck this.

Tim squashes in front of Billy.

Billy   Who ye fuckin pushin? Did they no teach manners in that Catholic school? Ever heard of please excuse me?

Tim   I don't beg – specially off Orangemen.

Billy   No but your starvin ancestors did. (*Tim lunges at Billy but Billy puts a palm out and points up at the camera*) And get this – see if that camera wasn't there, I'd take your fuckin heid aff.

Tim   Don't be too sure, fatty – I boxed for years.

Billy   Is that what it is? I thought ye were born ugly. Ye've got a face oan ye like thon cunt oot the Pogues.

Tim   I might be ugly but you're daft an in the mornin I'll be... I'll be...

Billy   Ha! Fuck – he canny even get that right. It's sober – you're ugly an I'll be sober in the mornin. Fuckin thicko!

Tim   Better watch it, pal. Wan day ye might come out frae work and I'll be waitin.

Billy splutters through his laughter.

Billy   I haven't got a joab, ya daft cunt. They sacked me!

Tim   Well – ye'll come out of somewhere.

Tim watches the game with Billy laughing and parodying Tim.

Billy   Aye – wan day ye'll come out fae work an I'll be waitin..

Tim ignores him and concentrates on the game a beat, then:

Tim   We're all over youse!

But Billy is thinking.

Billy   Aye right! Hey wait a minute – what was that ye sayed aboot me talkin through ma arse? About bein British?

Tim   Ye sayed ye would support Scotland.

Billy   Aye?

Tim   And ye've got that fuckin Union Jack on yer arm – not to mention the big poof on the white horse.

Billy   The Union Jack's in solidarity wi ma

brothers across the water.

Tim   What water? The Clyde?

Billy No – no the fuckin Clyde – in Belfast. And that's a lot of shite aboot King Billy bein a poof.

Tim   You're as daft as ye said I was. On wan hand yer sayin ye support Scotland but on the other arm – ye support a united Britain. Fuck they even sing 'Rule Britannia' at Ibrox. Govan for fuck sakes! They sing about crushin the Scots in that song.

Billy No that's in 'God Save The Queen'.

Tim   Well then – there ye fuckin go! Politics.

Billy You know nothin aboot the politics behind it aw.

Tim   There's only wan person in here knows nothin about the politics behind it.

Billy I know!

Tim   It's dangerous, ye know. Look what happened in Bosnia!

Billy Bosnia? Oh ho. Fuck sake, he's away in Bosnia noo.

Tim   Have your fuckin turn.

Tim goes to the lavvy pan. Billy goes to the hatch and watches for a beat then starts humming, then singing: moving towards Tim is trying not to laugh.

Billy   Singin I'm no a Croat I'm a Serb,
        Singin I'm no a Croat I'm a Serb,
        Singin I'm no a Croat, I'm no a Croat,
        I'm no a Croat I'm a Serb.

Tim eventually laughs. Billy goes and lies on the bench. Harry comes back in – checks the phone.

Tim   Ha ha very funny – for a Proddy.

Billy   Aye – we've got the craic wi the best of them, ye know.

Tim   Aw, wait a minute!

Billy   What?

Tim   You used an Irish word there.

Billy   What?

Tim   Craic.

Billy   And?

Tim   I think you've got Catholic blood in ye.

Billy   Have I fuck!

Tim   An ye used another word earlier on. But I let that go.

Billy   What would I be doin usin Oirish words?

Tim   That's jist what I was askin myself.

A beat, then:

Billy   What word?

Tim   Oul. Ye sayed *oul* cars. Ye got done for ringin *oul* cars.

Billy   And that should interest me because?

Tim   Because – it's only Irish immigrants that use that word.

Billy   Are you sayin I'm a fuckin tattie howker?

Tim   Aye. (*chants*) Fenian, Fenian (*pointing*) Fenian, Fenian… Dirty Fenian bastard… dirty Fenian bastard…

Billy ignores Tim. Eventually Tim sickens and stops.

6

Harry is sitting in a formal position. We come to see that he's actually preparing for prayer. Billy sees him and goes to the hatch.

Harry   I know I've not done this since I was a laddie. But it's not for me. It's for the wean. If you can see your way to making sure he's alright. That's all I want. You can take me instead. I'd gladly get hit by a bus or a heart attack or whatever. (*Harry listens as if for an answer then readjusts his position and his tone into something much more formal – palms out*) Our Father, who art in heaven, hallowed be thy name…

Tim   Dirty Fenian bastard…

Billy   Shht!

Tim   Dirty Fenian bastard…

Billy   Shht!

Tim   What?

Billy   C'mere!

Tim comes to the hatch.

Tim   What is it?

Billy   He's prayin. Must be bad.

Billy and Tim share a concerned look.

Tim   Canny hear fuck all.

Billy   He's stopped. Was definitely prayin but.

They listen for a beat, then:

Tim   (*Whisper*) Who's turn is it?

Billy   That's half-time anyhow.

Harry is preparing the coffee.

Tim   Fuck.

Billy   Neck's killin iz lookin through that hatch.

Tim   Mine an all.

Billy   An ma ears.

Tim   Ears?

Billy   You've geed them some bashin the whole first half.

Tim snorts a laugh at that.

Tim   An you never? (*beat*) Aye – ye're right. Ma head's spinnin – gettin lifted first thing an then all this. (*beat*)

Billy   Fuck it. Ceasefire then?

Tim   Ceasefire?

Billy   Fuckin truce. We're as well – we're in this thegether.

Tim considers this, then:

Tim   Okay.

But they don't now what to do now they're in truce mode. They sit and think a beat, then Harry comes in.

Harry   Here ye go, boys. Half-time, lads. Cup of coffee for yees. Sorry there's no Bovril. (*Harry hands two cups of coffee through*) Sugar and milk was already in it.

Tim   Thanks man – I'm Hank Marvin.

Billy   So am I. I could chew the tyres aff a bus.

Tim laughs at that. Harry is trying for a signal.

Tim   I could eat a scabby horse between two pishy matresses.

Billy laughs at that.

Billy   Starvin Harry – if my bum could munch I'd eat wi that an all.

Harry   I'll send out for a couple of sausage suppers if you're still in the night.

Tim   Christ I hope not.

Harry   Hey. I need you out too. I've got things to do.

Harry goes into a dwam.

Tim   Wan of us'll be out anyway.

Billy   Harry?

Harry   Aye?

Billy   Ye all right?

Harry   Aye. (*emotional beat*) No. No really. Ach – it's my wee grandson. My boy's wean. He in for a big operation the now. Heart.

He's only four.

Billy Fuck – I hope he's alright Harry.

Tim He'll be fine.

Harry I feel he will be myself – but it's the waiting.

Tim These guys know what they're doin.

Billy Aye – fuck – it's an everyday occurrence to them.

Harry Suppose it is.

Tim Like you in here – if somebody's up the court for the first time an in the cells, they're probably shitin theirselves – but to you it's yer job – an everyday... (*looks to Billy*)

B/T Occurrence.

Tim Aye, occurrence. Every day occurrence.

Harry Better get back in case they phone.

Harry goes out.

Tim Is he takin it bad? Yer son?

Harry It's my daughter-in-law I'm talking to. My son hasn't spoke to me in years.

Tim   How's that?

Billy gives Tim a poke in the ribs with his elbow. Harry closes the door and walks away.

Billy   Harry!

Harry turns – goes to the hatch.

Harry   Aye son?

Hold the stare for a long time, then:

Billy   Thanks for the coffee eh!

Harry nods his head cos he can't speak. He goes.

Tim   See! See! Told ye there was somethin wrong – I'm great at listenin to phone calls, me, so I am.

Billy   You're a prick!

Tim   What?

Billy   Askin about his son like that.

Tim   Was only makin conversation, man. (*Billy shakes his head and they both sip their coffee*) He'll be okay.

Billy   Aye.

Silent beats.

Tim   But what d'ye think his son's not talkin to him for?

Billy shrugs.

Billy   Fuck knows. Could be anythin. (*Billy comes and sits down*) Families, man.

Silent beats. They think of their home life.

7

Billy   She's probably took the weans for a burger. Know – if she's went up the Halifax.

Tim   What've ye got weans-wise?

Billy   Two. Lassie at five – wee boy at three.

Tim   I'm the same. Lassie at five and laddie at four. (*silence as they look at each other surreptitiously perhaps as human beings for the first time – empathy is setting in*) So ye got the sack?

Billy   Eh?

Tim   Ye were sayin earlier on ye got the sack.

Billy   Aye.

Tim   Where d'ye work?

Billy   I was a hairdresser.

Tim   (*amused*) A fuckin hairdresser's. Ye do not look like a fuckin hairdresser.

Billy   What does a hairdresser look like?

Tim   (*shrugging*) So what happened?

Billy   I hate it. Most of the customers work in the telly and the theatre. Know; black polo neck shaved heads wee poofy black bags? The boss forces me to talk with this posh accent. This woman came in and she's gave me stick a few times before. This day she gave me abuse (*posh Glasgow accent*) Excuse me could you get my bags from my car – thank you! It's not how it's why. Please! Would you speak the Queen's English. Then she asks what could I do to make her look younger. (*using Tim as a customer*) I'll tell you what – a wee tint of titian here, bit of copper there – a trim. And if that doesn't work I'll get you a bed in a geriatric fuckin hospital. (*Tim bursts out laughing at that*) I'd been dyin to say that for ages.

Tim   Fuck sake – what did she say?

Billy   Fuckin left in tears.

Tim   Good on ye man. Fuck her. Snobby cow.

Fuckin deserved it. They're always on about us – sectarianism eh – but we're not the only sectarianism Scotland's got.

Billy Tell me about it – Poofy bastard of a boss sacked me. (*Billy impersonates his poofy boss*) That was simply deplorable, William.

Billy puts his hand on Tim's leg.

Tim (*withdrawing*) Haw!

Billy I'm afraid I'll have to let you go. (*when Tim's stopped laughing*) So. Well, what about you?

Tim Eh?

Billy Come on. Where d'you work?

Tim Call centre. Cos we talk that wee bit posher than normal, us Tims. Know – fuckin shop instead of shoap. House instead of fuckin hoose.

Billy Is it any good?

Tim Shite. Ye just talk to people all day about credit ratings. Get hunners of abuse an all.

Billy Aye, I bet they don't ask if you're a Tim or a Hun there.

Tim Not when it comes to money. (*They think about that then*) Coffee tastes amazin in here so it does.

Billy An when ye're away campin.

Tim That's right so it does right enough. Where did ye go?

Billy is dreaming as Tim takes a drink.

Billy Donegal! (*Tim splurges his coffee all over Billy's Rangers top, laughing*) I jist bought this ya wank!

Tim How the fuck did ye end up in Donegal?

Billy I was a laddie.

Tim But how come ye ended up there?

Billy I don't know do I? My Da took iz.

Tim Fuck – you're wan for the watchin.

Billy (*wiping his top with the sash*) Fuckin prick – look at that.

Tim Oh I've got my beady eye on you sir.

Billy throws the sash at Tim.

Billy Keep your beady eye on that.

Harry   (*knocking at the door*) Second half's starting, lads!

Tim   Thanks, Harry.

Billy   Ta, mate.

Tim   Heard anythin?

Harry shakes his head.

Harry   No, nothing.

8

Tim and Billy acknowledge Harry's pain as Harry walks away, a worried man. Billy goes up to the hatch – Billy and Tim could be two friends now.

Billy   Easy, Walter the genius Smith versus that wee wank Strachan!

Tim   Right here's one for you then. Hey who's this!? (*Tim does an impersonation of a drunk Donald Findlay*) Oh the cry was no surrender… If M'Lud be pleased on behalf of the accused wink wink level, level how's your granny's wooden leg on the square.

Billy   (*getting it*) Donald Findlay. (*as judge*) Donald Findlay? You stand here accused of sectarian acts – not to mention your really dodgy singin voice. How do you plead.

Tim   Like this, m'lud.

Tim stands in the Masonic distress stance: his heels together, his feet at right angles, his left hand shielding his eyes from the sun his right hand straight as a poker by his side.

Billy (*to Tim*) Aah! (*as judge*) Donald Findlay – you are allegedly a Mason. Get your arse out of here!

Tim marches away singing.

Tim (*as Donald Findlay*) Oh the cry was no surrender!!! (*Billy can't stop laughing. Tim watches Billy laugh for a beat, then*) D'ye know the worst thing about it but?

Billy What?

Tim Wanny youse bastards stuck him in. The guy was only enjoyin hisself.

Billy I know. He even got hunners of letters from Tims.

Tim An what about that joke he done in Belfast?

Billy The smoke?

Tim Fuck! (*doing Findlay*) It's awful fuckin smoky in here – has another fuckin Pope died? (*both laugh, then*) How's it illegal to sing sectarian songs in a country full of bigots?

Billy   Fuck knows? (*stamps his foot*) One two three – Altogether now – The cry was no surrender…

Tim joins in loud. Harry crashes to the hatch.

Harry   Right lads – that's it – telly's going off.

Billy   No, wait.

Tim   We were just having a laugh Harry!

Harry   It's going off.

Billy   Harry! It was a joke man!

Harry   Can't hear myself think.

Tim   Come on Harry.

Harry   I'm not listening to that bliddy racket.

Harry's hand is on the hatch.

Billy   We'll calm down Harry – oan the square – (*Billy holds Harry's hand*) Come oan Harry.

Harry   No more noise – promise? (*beat*) This is your last chance. I've enough to worry about without the likes of this.

Billy   Sorry Harry. (*Harry leaves. Tim stares at Billy with a knowing look*) What's up wi you?

Tim   Mmm mm.

Billy   What?

Tim   Mm mm.

Billy   What ye lookin at me like that for?

Tim   Aye! Oh aye! I can see it all clear as fuck now.

Billy   What is it?

Tim   Ceasefire's over, mate.

Billy   What are you oan?

Tim   Not the square anyway.

Billy   The square?

Tim   I should've knew earlier – I mean, how's a turnkey goanny let us watch the fuckin telly?

Billy   He *is* lettin us watch the fuckin telly.

Tim   Exactly.

Billy   Oh – you're freakin me oot ya fuckin weirdo! (*Tim still stares at Billy in that unnerving way*) What? (*Tim still stares*) What is it!!?

Tim   You gave that cunt the handshake!

Billy   The handshake?

Tim   Don't gimmi it! – the two of yees – all that level and square shite – admit it.

Billy   I'm admittin nothin.

Tim   Right. (*shouts*) Harry – ye're a fuckin Mason!!

Billy   Shh – ya insensitive cunt. His grandson's no well.

Tim   (*quiet*) Ye stuck yer hand out that hatch an gave him the tickly finger – that's how he's lettin us watch the game.

Billy   I'm not in the fuckin Masons!

Tim   Aye ye are. Yees all join them to get on. At our expense!

Billy   At your expense?

Tim   Aye – our expense.

Billy   The Masons aren't even anti-Catholic!

Tim   Aye! I know – ye can join them if ye're a Catholic – so long as ye stop bein a Catholic!

Billy   Why don't yous stop bein Catholics then – assimilate! It's a Proddy country.

Tim   I don't want to assimilate. I want to (*searches for the word*) integrate.

Billy   What's the fuckin difference.

Tim   Well – we get to keep our culture!

Billy   You keep twistin it round to culture.

Tim   Assimilate's like that big fuckin spaceship thing in *Star Wars* that swallows everythin up. Integrate is to fit in right, like a bit of a jigsaw! That's what I want to do. Be a bit of the jigsaw that makes up Scotland.

Tim walks away, proud of his eloquence.

Billy   Spaceship?

Tim   Aye!

Billy   Here have another tattie.

Tim   How fuckin can I – you et them all!

They ignore each other a beat, then:

Billy   Right! Listen. Lets say I gave him the handshake.

Tim   A—haa!

Billy   I'm not sayin I gave him the handshake. I'm sayin, let's imagine I gave him the handshake. We're gettin to watch the fuckin game are we no?

Tim   I'm not acceptin charity frae no on-the-square-fiddle-ma-middle-digit-sheepskin-wearin-goat-buckin-Mason.

Billy   Fine well.

Tim   Good.

Billy   Fine.

Tim   Good.

Billy   I'll watch it.

Tim   Watch it well.

Tim takes the huff as Billy goes to hatch and takes up position.

Billy   We are aw over youse. (*Tim shrugs*) Oh. Fuckin hell man. What's happened to youse this half? (*Tim tries to peer past Billy*) Thought ye didn't accept charity.

Tim   Fuck off.

Billy   Whao! An inch over the bar, that was.

Tim can't stand it and shoves Billy out the way to take his turn at the hatch.

Tim   Right out the way. It's my turn.

Billy lifts his left trouser leg at Tim.

Billy   Okay, brother.

Tim   I'll fuckin brother ye!

Billy   Okay, brother.

Tim   I want ye to know that acceptin this doesn't mean I'm on the level or on the square or whatever fuckin shape youse cunts are.

Billy   Right.

Tim   Right.

Billy   (*lets Tim turn his back, then*) Brother.

Tim   (*Tim reacts then*) Come on Camara – into these (*rhythm of the old Coke advert*) Orange-Mason-hand-shakin-Ulster-lovin-finger-ticklin-Tim-hatin-goat-buckin-Proddy-fuckin-bastards.

Billy   That's no bad that by the way.

Tim   Eh!?

Tim, proud of himself, returns to the game.

Billy   Yees're shite without O'Neill.

Tim   I'll give ye that.

Tim watches the game. Billy sings low.

Billy   Hello – Hello – we are the Billy boys,
        Hello – Hello – you'll know us by our noise,
        We're up to our knees in Fenian blood...

Tim   Whoa whoa whoa. Stop right there. You're a great wan for the questions so ye are – can I ask wan now?

Billy   Fire away.

Tim   Right – you say Scotland's *not* an anti-Catholic country!

Billy   When did I say that?

Tim   When ye sayed I was paranoid.

Billy   Ye are. Aw Tims're para.

Tim   Would ye bet on that?

Billy   Aye –

Tim   Yer five hunner quid?

Billy   If I hadn't stuck it oan Rangers.

Tim   Would ye bet yer freedom on it but?

Billy   Aye.

Tim   Rangers win I get out with your winnings. You stay in?

Billy   If ye can prove Scotland's anti-Catholic – aye I sayed.

Tim   Right – Here's a wee song for ye then – listen to this –

Billy   I'm aw ears.

Tim   Hello – Hello – we are the Billy boys,
         (*Billy joins in*)
         Hello – Hello – you'll know us by our noise,
         We're to our knees in Paki blood,
         No – We're up to our knees in Darkie blood,
         No – We're up to our knees in Jewish blood.

Billy   Aw – fuck – you have lost it noo sir!

Tim   No – We're up to our knees in Chinkee blood,
         No – We're up our knees in Moslem blood.

Billy   Wham bam solid gone – away wi the fuckin bongos.

Tim   Bongos? Imagine singin up to our knees in Paki blood in England.

Billy   And?

Tim   You'd get lifted. Not to mention pure Abdulled an all. Boom!

Billy   You're talkin shite.

Tim   The whole crowd would get lifted.

Billy   Aye right!

Tim   The whole fuckin team!

Billy   Would we fuck.

Tim   It would be a national disgrace.

Billy   Aye right.

Tim   It *is* a national disgrace in fact.

Billy   Yous are a national disgrace!

Tim   How the fuck are we a national disgrace?

Billy   We work – you drink – we pay!

Tim   The team'd be banned an it'd be all over the ten o'clock news if it was England. Fuck – a couple of monkey noises and it's headlines. But yous can be up to yer knees in our Fenian blood?

A beat, then Billy comes up with:

Billy   We're singin about the Fenian Brotherhood – see. It's a historical song.

Tim   Oh aye – sixty-thousand Rangers fans're suddenly university-educated historians. (*Billy tries to answer but can't*) Youse cunts sing it every week an it's on the telly. Hello – Hello – we are the Billy boys, Hello – Hello ye'll know us by our noise, we're up to our knees in (*Indicating himself*) Fenian blood. *Tim walks away vindicated.*

A beat, then:

Billy   Glory glory what a hell of away to die, (*rises and goes towards Tim*) glory glory what a hell of a way to die, (*Tim tries to interrupt and Billy stops him*) glory glory what a hell of a way to die, to die an Orange bastard!

Tim   Fair play. (*a beat then*) But – you've got to admit it Billy – us Tims've contributed a fuckin lot to this country.

Billy   What? Tatties? Fuckin junkies? Alkies? Prisoners?

Tim   No. Patter! Fuckin fun! Smiles. What a dour

>   country this would be without us! (*dour voice*) Hello, welcome to Scotland. The land with a lot of fun in it. (*stands*) We abuse dead Popes! (*blesses himself*) Rest in peace John Paul. Aye – the land with a lot of fun. Scotland – a laugh a minute!

Billy   So yees laughed once. Big fuckin waw! Is that it?

Tim   No that's not it! Canals – roads – motorways – iron – steel – fuckin Celtic!

Billy yawns feigning boredom.

Billy   Anythin else? Cuddly toy?

Tim   What have youse cunts ever gave Scotland?

Billy   Let me see now. Polis. Law and order. Armies. The fuckin Scottish Enlightenment.

Tim   The what?

Billy   Free fuckin thinkin – scientific thinkin, man – fuckin telly, the phone – half the ships in the world at one time.

Tim   Aye, an many Catholics worked in the shipyards?

Billy   That was years ago.

Tim   An it's still the same.

Billy   So an it is!

Tim   It fuckin is.

Billy   That right? You try getting a job in Glasgow Council if you're a Proddy. (*Tim is caught out*) Well?

Tim   Right enough. Quite fuckin right!

Billy   Fuck sake, Tim, Scotland's not just anti-Catholic – it's anti-Christian. Ye can be a Moslem a Hindu or a Buddhist. Ye can be a fuckin sandal-eater or a whale-shagger and everybody respects ye – treats ye with kid gloves, fuckin goes oot their way to make sure ye can practise your religion. But as soon as you say ye're a Christian of any kind – they fuckin laugh at ye! They think ye're fuckin mad! Ye can get locked up in the loony bin in this country, oor fuckin country, just for bein a Christian!

Tim   Ye're spot-on, by the way. (*Tim thinks about it*) See for a Hun, Billy – you're pretty bright.

Billy   (*pride*) Aye! The future's bright. The future's Orange.

Tim laughs. Billy laughs. They sit in silence, thinking.

9

Harry's phone rings. Harry comes running back in and grabs it. Tim crashes against the door – listening. Billy joins him.

Harry   Harry here. Is he okay? Is everything alright? No. No. (*shock*) For God sakes.

Tim   Fuck!

Harry   I thought they were supposed to be professionals? Sorry, hen – I know – it's just...

Tim   Somethin's went wrong.

Harry   Did they get his weight right? They might've weighed him wrong? Aw, God.

Tim   (*to Billy*) C'mere!

Harry   Right. Right. Soon as you hear anything.

Billy   Poor cunt.

Harry   Anything at all. (*beat*) Me too. I've been praying all day. Okay hen. You go back in. Tell him his grandad's thinking about him. Just say it to him anyway. Can you not get Bobby to talk to me? This *is* a crisis! What've I got to do to get him to talk to me? My own son.

Tim and Billy listen. The phone clicks off and Harry lets his arm descend blindly to the table. His shoulders go up and down in big sobs. Tim and Billy listen to Harry crying a beat then:

Billy   He's greetin.

Tim   (*to get off the Harry subject*) Mon. Just, eh, crack on wi the game.

Billy   Fuck the game.

Billy sits down. Tim sits down. After a few beats:

Tim   So?

Billy   What?

Tim   Did I win the bet?

Billy   Aye. Phone ma wife and tell her no to

bother payin ma fine. Jist pay the Tim's. Yes that's right dear – the Tim's!

Tim But d'ye not get what I mean?

Billy Aboot what?

Tim Up to our knees in Fenian blood an that.

Billy Mibbi.

Tim Come on – throw me a fuckin tattie here at least! I've got a point, eh?

Billy Mibbi!

Tim Mibbi?

Billy A wee bit!

Tim Mibbi a wee bit?

Billy Ye've goat a wee bit of a point.

Tim (*emotional*) Thanks.

Billy (*to himself*) Aw for fuck sakes. (*to Tim*) What's up? You're not goanny start greetin now are ye?

Tim No. It's just… it's just… that's the first I've ever heard a Hun admittin anythin like that. (*Tim looks at Billy deciding to tell him or not)* Listen – I've never told anybody this but…

Billy You a poof?

Tim Don't tell no cunt this by the way…

Billy Aw no – he is a poof.

Tim No – see sometimes when Rangers're in Europe – I want them to win – I cheer them on.

Billy Aye right yar! An the new Pope flings the stick in the walk at Brigton Cross.

Tim No – I do – cos they're a Scottish team. See a couple of years ago when Rangers were playin Stuttgart?

Billy I was at that game.

Tim I was watchin it on the box. Rootin for Rangers. I used to wonder, all the time I'd been supportin Rangers in Europe, if mibbi I'm jist doin this to make myself feel good. Kiddin myself on. Anyway I can't right remember the score but Rangers needed a goal. See when they scored? I fuckin leaps up aff the couch an shouted On the Gers! Honest to fuck, I was in mid air when I realised I wasn't a bigot.

Billy   Ye jumped up?

Tim   Like that! Mid-air I was in – like that – (*demonstrates*) cross ma heart hope to die.

Billy   (*elation*) Jist think – we were in mid-air at the same time. (*a thought*) If you're tellin the truth.

Beat, then:

Tim   I am tellin the truth! Look – I think everybody's a bigot. We've all got bigotry. Every single person's got bigotry for somethin. I can prove it.

Billy   You can prove everythin. You should be a fuckin scientist.

Tim   See when I landed after cheerin the Rangers? Just as my arse hit the couch? I shouted, (*shouts*) Gerrit up yees, ya German bastards! See! See! (*Billy laughs*) Ma bigotry jist shifted on to somethin else! Gerrit up yees, ya fuckin Nazis! (*When they stop laughing*) D'you never feel like that for Celtic. When we're in Europe I mean?

Billy thinks a beat then goes to the bench – pats it.

Billy   Right. Grab a seat. (*Tim sits*) See when Celtic were in the UEFA cup final?

Tim   (*reverie*) Seville!

Billy   I goat barred out JJB Sports in Sauchiehall street.

Tim   For what?

Billy   Tryin to buy a Porto scarf.

Tim   No fuckin way!

Billy   Any Porto scarves mate I said. The guy laughed. I'm serious, I goes. He goes, are you sick or somethin? He wasn't even a Tim, he says. In fact he had a season ticket for Ibrox.

Tim   That's fuckin sick that, by the way!

Billy   (*amused*) I know! (*Billy laughs a beat then*) Porto Porto. (*Tim is disappointed and shows it*) Porto Porto. (*continues*)

Billy eventually sickens at his own bigotry, stops.

Tim   (*hurt*) It's your turn.

Billy goes to the hatch filling up with guilt.

Billy   Come oan Rae ya big fanny! (*apologetically to Tim*) He's a fuckin big fanny him. (*Tim ignores him*) Aw, fuck, Tim. Aw this shite… It's a safety valve, in't it.

Rangers and Celtic – for hate.

Tim You shouldn't need a fuckin safety valve but, should ye?

Billy I know. (*beat*) Well what do you want to do aboot it?

Tim I don't fuckin know, do I.

Billy I do?

A beat, then:

Tim Go, well!

Billy Right. First ye merge Rangers an Celtic.

Tim Merge them? Ye mad?

Billy How's that?

Tim Nobody'd stand for it.

Billy What would you do?

Tim Fuckin leave.

Billy Me too.

Tim Well, what ye on about then?

Billy Guys like you and me. The bigots. That's

        who'd leave. But this big new team. Call it anythin ye like. Glasgow United, or whatever. Aw the Rangers an Celtic fans that's no bigots – they'd stay behind an support the team!

Tim   (*dreaming of football glory*) It'd be some team right enough.

Billy   Up there wi Barcelona and Man U.

Tim   Ah but then we'd really fuck all the wee teams. An that would fuck Scottish football.

Billy   Aha! That's where part two of the plan comes into action. Right. Think about it! Where would aw the bigots go?

Tim   The pub?

Billy   The pub? The fuckin pub? Efter the pub, ya maniac!

Tim   Home.

Billy   (*exasperated*) I mean where would they put their bigotry? (*Tim shrugs*) They'd go to other teams.

Tim shoots his hand up and answers like a school kid who just thought of the answer.

Tim   Hearts an Hibs!

Billy   Hearts an Hibs. Then what would happen to them?

Tim   Donno.

Billy   They'd become big teams like Rangers and Celtic. Powered an funded by bigotry!

Tim   So they would. But not as big as Glasgow United.

Billy   No. No till ye merged Hearts an Hibs an aw. Then they become a big team in Europe an what happens next?

Tim   How the fuck do I know? It's you that's makin it up.

Billy   The bigots find two other teams. Pump their money an bigotry into them. Then what?

Tim   (*bright*) They – two – teams – merge!

Billy   Exactly – and ye keep doin that till even Albion Rovers are playin in Europe. (*Tim is enthralled by Billy's evangelising*) We can save oor nation with bigotry. Eh? Eh?

Tim   Fuck! Fuck! That's a good idea Billy Boy! (*Tim thinks about it*) It's a good fuckin idea!

Tim's face falls as Billy crashes back down to earth.

Billy   But that's a fuckin dream though int it? No cunt looks like scorin.

Tim   Time to call the cavalry.

Tim kneels down and blesses himself, facing Billy.

Billy   What the fuck ye doin?

Tim   Prayin for Celtic to score.

Tim prays on.

Billy   Goanny mumble quieter. Geen me the creeps.

Tim finishes his prayers and stands up throwing Billy a right smug you're-done-for-now look. Tim indicates God.

Tim   Aye – yous are done for now.

Billy   Whoah ho!

Tim   That's ma lucky prayer.

Billy   Fuckin lucky prayer!

Tim   We'll see.

Billy   We will see. (*Billy goes to the hatch. Let's*

*out noise after noise as Celtic's goal is
assailed*) Novo. Novo. Ferguson. Novo!
Boyd (*silent tick*) Yesssssssss!!! Goal.
(*Billy dances round the cell*) Boyd! Ya fuckin
beauty! Take that ya Fenian cunts. Wan nil.

Harry looks at the telly, looks in the cell, shakes his head.

Tim   Fuck!!!

Billy   Where's yer God noo?

Tim   Thought he was a big fanny? Boyd?

Billy   Wi a heid oan him like that? Naw!
(*Billy sings low*)
I'm free – I'm free –
I'm free to leave this cell –
I leave behind a Fenian cunt –
roastin in his pish –
we are the Brigton Billy boys...

Tim   Celtic can still score – there's ten minutes left.

Billy   Whoah ho there's wan Tim who won't be oot oan the streets tonight.

Tim   There's ten minutes left.

Billy   What was that prayer again? I'll need to try it oot myself wan day, when the chips are down. Goanny write it down for me.

10

Harry's phone rings. Tim and Billy crash to the cell door. Harry grabs the phone.

Harry Bobby? (*his face falls*) Oh – no sorry – I was waiting on a call there from somebody else. What's that. Okay – wait till I get a pen. (*Harry gets a pen and a bit of paper*) Fire away.

Tim No – sounds like somethin official just.

Harry writes something down and he smiles as he does despite the pain that he's in.

Harry Right... right... right... okay.

Tim is watching the game and ad-libbing.

Billy I'll be thinkin aboot ye when I'm in the Orange Hall wi ma mates the night.

Bang bang bang – the door goes. It's Harry. He has a piece of notepaper in his hand. Billy and Tim go to the hatch.

Harry   Tim – message from your wife.

Tim takes the note and flips it this way and that. Harry hangs about too long.

Tim   Cheers Harry. Any news yet?

Harry tries to talk but can't.

Billy   Aye, one nil to us!

Harry   Bit of bad news there. Bad reaction to the anaesthetic.

Billy   I'm sorry, Harry.

Harry   The operation went great – but...

Billy   Jesus, Harry.

Harry   I've been praying all day.

Billy   Harry – we'll say a wee prayer – eh Tim? (*to Harry*) If that's alright?

Harry   Would youse, lads? Can only help, eh?

Billy   No problem. Tim?

Tim   (*dying to read the note*) Aye.

Harry   Thanks lads. I've got to be near a phone!

Harry goes back to his office and stares at the phone. Tim and Billy avoid looking at each other cos they know they have to pray as promised.

Tim   Poor cunt.

Billy   I know. Imagine it was wan of oor weans.

They scour the cell a few beats.

Tim   Aye.

Billy   Aye.

A few beats more.

Tim   I'll eh... (*Tim walks to one corner. But he doesn't do anything*) I can't wi you fuckin lookin at me, can I. Goanny turn away or somethin.

Billy walks over solemnly to Tim.

Billy   Don't use that prayer ye used earlier for fuck sakes.

Tim   (*smiling*) Don't worry.

After each of them check the other one isn't

watching they begin – as quietly as they can.

Billy   Dear Lord, a prayer for Harry's grandson. He say his name?

Tim   No. (*Tim blesses himself*) Hail Mary, full of grace, the Lord is with thee. Blessed are thou among women and blessed is the fruit of thy womb, Jesus.

Tim notices Billy bowing his head.

Billy   Dear Lord a prayer for Harry's grandson that everythin goes okay in his operation.

Tim   Holy Mary Mother of God, pray for us sinners now and at the hour of our death amen.

When Tim and Billy finish praying they sit down embarrassed, and Tim unfolds the letter. Billy watches closely as he reads every line and then reads it again. Flips it this way and that. Tim doesn't know what to make of it.

Billy   What is it?

Tim   Nothin.

Billy   A love letter?

Tim   It's nothin.

Billy hugs Tim.

Billy   Come oan – ye can tell yer big Proddy pal.

Tim   Leave me!

Tim pulls away from Billy.

Billy   Gimmi!

Billy grabs the letter from Tim. Tim grabs it back with violence.

Tim   Fuckin gimmi it!!

Billy   Whoa!!

Tim   It's a fuckin private letter.

Billy   Was only havin a laugh!

Tim   Jist leave me alone – eh?

Billy   What happened to that famous Tim sense of humour?

Tim   There I'll show ye. (*stuffs the letter in his pocket*) In there, ya prick.

Billy feels chastised. He tries to please Tim. Tim goes and lies down.

Billy   Here – it's your turn. (*Tim ignores him*) It's

your turn to watch the game.

Tim   You watch it.

Beat. Billy doesn't know what to do.

Billy   But it's your turn.

Tim slumps down onto the bed.

Tim   You take ma turn, I sayed.

Billy   Celtic might still score.

Tim   So what.

Billy   Ye can't lie there at a time like this. Who am I going to gloat over?

Tim   I'm goin to sleep – right!

Billy   How the fuck can ye?

Tim   I'm goin to sleep.

11

Billy watches Tim/the game for a bit then, in a pique, lies down and huffs and puffs like the angry wife.

Tim   Fuck sake. (*Tim looks up and sees Billy*) What ye doin?

Billy   It's no use without an enemy, is it. Come on, get up there an start shoutin.

Tim   I don't want ma turn I sayed.

Billy   That's jist like youse Fenians. When yer team's winnin yees're aw singin aw dancin. But soon as yees're gettin beat, yees gie up.

Tim   Eh – I can hear ye – that's Rangers fans that do that.

Billy   You're doin it the now.

Billy mutters on like a scorned wife huffing and puffing and turning, until:

Tim Fuck! (*Tim stands up and looks out through the hatch*) I'm up. There – happy?

Billy Yes.

Tim Come on, McGeady, pass it ya wee Irish cunt ye. (*Tim jumps up screaming as Celtic score*) McDonald! Oh ya fuckin beau—t—y

Tim trails off as he speaks – his mood dipping.

Billy Aw, fuck! Fuck! Fuck! (*When Billy recovers he notices that Tim's face has suddenly and inexplicably fallen*) What's up wi ye now? Celtic jist scored. Ye're quiet.

Tim I know I'm quiet, I can hear myself.

Billy A draw – that's no bad for everybody. Aw round. (*Billy realises the implications of a draw*) Aw fuck!

Tim (*quick change of tone to worry*) What?

Billy A draw! That does no cunt fuck-aw good that, does it? (*On Tim realising*) If it stays like this we're both stayin in here, mate!

Tim Aye, an if Celtic never scored we were both gettin out! (*Billy stares at Tim puzzling*)

>   Here. (*Tim hands Billy the note*) The wife.
>   She put the fuckin money on Rangers to
>   win, ma wife, so she did.

Billy   Ye're fuckin kiddin?

Billy reads. Slowly – as if holding it in – Billy lets go a laugh and can't stop. Slowly again – Tim is infected by Billy's laughter.

Tim   She put the money oan fuckin Rangers!

Billy   She put the fuckin money oan Rangers!

Tim   Mental, in't it? Some bastard at the bookies
          told her Rangers were the better team.
          Nightmare.

Billy   She put the fuckin money oan Rangers!

Tim   She put the money oan fuckin Rangers!
          That's it! Fuckin divorce!

A roar from the telly.

Billy   That's it. It's over. Wan each.

Tim   Fuckin great! Now we're worse off than we
          were when we came in.

Billy is trying to be sarcastic but failing.

Billy   At least I made a big Fenian pal!

Tim   Aye – fuckin right!

But they are intensely awkward at the truth beneath that. To cover, Billy starts gently bumping into Tim.

Billy   For it's a grand old team to go to jail for,
Sure it's a grand old team to pay the bail for, for if – you know – the history…

Tim bursts in.

Tim   Hello – Hello – we are the Billy boys,
Hello – Hello – You'll know us by our noise…

Harry is about to shout in when Billy stops and offers him his shirt.

Billy   Here, ya cunt.

Tim   Fuck off!

Billy   Come on, ya big ride.

Tim   No fuckin way.

Billy   Come on, take it! Ye'll offend me!

Tim   Ach!

Tim takes the shirt – they swap, making a big thing of it. Ad-libbing.

Billy   Don't tell no cunt, by the way!

Tim   Horrible!

Billy   Phew it's true what they say about youse soap dodgers.

Tim   Burnin my skin.

Billy   Aye. That'll be the detergent.

They adjust and admire each other's tops.

Billy   Suits you.

Tim   Fuck off!

Billy   Derek fuckin Johnston!

Tim looks down at his Rangers top then starts singing with great gusto.

Tim   Weeeeeeee're up to our knees in Fenian blood, (*Billy joins in*)
Surrender or you'll die,
We are the Brigton Billy boys.
HELLO – HELLO –
We are the Billy boys…
(*they sing on – loud*)

12

At the racket Harry gets up and is about to go to the cell when his phone rings.

Harry   Hello? (*shouts*) Boys! Boys! Shut up youse two, will yees I'm on the fuckin phone here! Christ! What? Oh – oh that's fantastic news.

B/T   Yaasss!

Harry   I'm relieved. (*stunned*) Bobby said that? Did he?

Tim   Bobby an all!

Billy   Mm mm.

Harry   What did he say? What? Hold on I can't hear you. Can we? Will we? Did he say that?

Tim   He's goanny meet him! Bobby's goanny

meet him.

Harry That's great, hen. Thanks for persuading him. When? Half an hour? No – half-an-hour is fine.

Harry puts the phone down. His warm smile changes to tears of relief. He thinks. Looks at his watch. Starts tidying up. Goes off. Tim looks out the cell.

Tim He's fucked off. Ye know something – even in that top you still look like a Proddy.

Billy An you still look like E.T.

Tim No – I mean it. Yous've all got wee fat necks an round shoulders, youse Proddies – no offence like!

Billy None taken – an yous're aw wiry – built for diggin roads an knockin weans oot yer wummin. No offence.

Tim But look at ye – all that's missin's the bowler hat an the sash.

Billy That's a lot of shite.

Tim Is it?

Billy Aye!

Tim   Aye! Ye can't change genetics.

Billy   Can ye no?

Tim   Scientific fact.

Billy   You're talkin through your arse.

Tim   D'ye think so?

Billy   I know so! I could prove it.

Tim   Prove it, then.

Billy   I could prove it.

Tim   Aye?

Billy   Fuckin shock ye!

Tim   Shock me, well!

Billy bursts forth.

Billy   Cos ma maw and da were Catholics ya fuckin dobber!

Tim chokes.

Tim   Now ye are talkin shite!

Billy   No – they split up – ma da was a right Fenian bastard – every Celtic game – right roon the world. Blew aw the money oan it. Like a fuckin addiction.

Tim　No fuckin way.

Billy　Every fuckin way – so when he left for a wee Irish burd – his Rose of Tralee – ma maw called her the Hoor of Tipperary – she brung me up a Rangers fan. Just to fuckin sicken him.

Tim stares at Billy a few beats then:

Tim　Ha! I knew ye had Tim blood in ye – that's what I sayed – didn't I – didn't I!!? What did I say?

Billy　Ye're a lyin cunt – ye jist sayed I was a picture perfect Proddy!

Tim　No, when ye said *oul* and then *craic* – I knew it!

Billy　Oh aye – that's right – so ye did – ye're a genius.

Billy sits beside Tim.

Tim　And – I seen ye bowin yer head when I was sayin the Hail Mary.

Billy　No ye never.

Tim　Ye did. I seen ye out the side of ma eyes.

	I was like that!?
Billy	Did ye fuck.
Tim	Automatic Catholic! Right enough see in this light – yer blue eyes've got a touch of Donegal blue – an yer neck – (*Tim puts his hands round Billy's neck and measures*) Not so fat after all.
Billy	So I'm no a fat Orange bastard any more?
Tim	Nothin a good diet an a bowlerhatectomy wouldn't fix.
Billy	So there ye go – aw yer shite aboot genetics.

Both sit in silence. Harry gets an idea. He takes out his credit card, lifts the phone again and dials a number.

Harry	Hi. Listen – do you accept credit cards?– (*continues giving out the number etc*)

Tim points at Billy.

Tim	(*sings*) Singin he's no a Billy, he's a Tim – Singin he's no a Billy, I'm a Tim –
Billy	(*sings*) Singin I'm no a Billy, he's a Tim – Singin I'm no a Billy, he's a Tim –

They sing to each other. Eventually, Tim, in elation,

stops Billy singing and blurts out:

Tim (*trying to force it out*) Listen... listen... Ma maw's a Proddy.

Billy Aw for fuck sakes – now you're makin it up.

Tim She is. Honest to God, cross ma heart, hope to die.

Billy You can't see shite go past ye. I tell ye I'm a Tim an you want to be a Proddy now. Ye'll be an Ulster Scot next.

Tim The whole family disowned ma maw when she married a Catholic. (*Tim is away in the past for a long time*) Ma da's family disowned him an all.

Billy Fuckin shite, in't it? My family disowned us first time one of them saw me doon the toon in a Rangers top.

Tim Quite fuckin right.

Billy I was fuckin six.

Tim Aw!

Billy falls into thought.

Billy Fuck sake, Tim — we're the only two cunts in here.

Tim   Eh, hello – I can see that!

Billy   That's what we've got in common.

Tim   What?

Billy   This – (*the cell*) us two – here! (*Billy walks to a corner*) It's like poetic justice! We're the only two in here, Tim. Can ye no see it?

Tim   Bumpin yer gums about?

Billy stands up and evangelises.

Billy   Right – the rest of the guys have got their fines paid.

Tim   Aye?

Billy   Why?

Tim   Cos their wifes got the money?

Billy   Where but? Where did they get the money?

Tim   Provvy cheque?

Billy   No a fuckin Provvy Cheque! They've obviously got their wifes to go roon their families and beg a tenner here – a fiver there. Can ye no see it?

Tim   See what?

Billy   There's nobody else in these cells but us. Tim! Come on ye must see it!?

Tim gets it suddenly.

Tim   Cos we've got nobody to get money off?

Billy   But why Tim? How've we got nobody? (*Tim shrugs*) Cos our families've disowned us.

Tim   Cos we're bigots?

Billy   No! Cos they're bigots, Tim! They are the fuckin bigots.

Tim   Ye're right Billy. Fuck – that's smart. I said it earlier and I'll say it again – for a half-baked Proddy ye've got a good head on ye so ye have. (*he thinks about it a beat, then*) Bastards!

Billy   Shake ma hand.

Tim   Fuck off.

Billy   Come on, shake ma fuckin hand!

Tim   No way!

Billy   We're goanny be in here thegether aw weekend – might as well start the peace process – shake.

Tim   Ach. (*They shake but Billy gives Tim the Masonic handshake*) Ach! Ya cunt! (*Billy is laughing*) Ya fucker. I knew ye were in the fuckin Masons!

Billy   Shh – it's a secret.

Tim checks for the all clear out the hatch then:

Tim   Wait till ye see what I've got down my secret sock, brother.

Tim reaches down his sock.

Billy   What is it, fags?

Tim   Better than fags.

Billy   Yer dick?

Tim   Ta naaa!

Tim produces a cracker of a joint.

Billy   A joint?

Tim   Popped it down ma sock when I seen the polis comin in the close.

Billy   Some spliff.

Tim pops the joint in Billy's mouth, sparks the lighter and lights the joint.

Tim   Be careful – there's a whole gram in that. (*Billy takes a long hard puff*) Peace be with you.

Billy   And also with you. (*They grin and point at each other*) Ahh!! That is a fuckin joint, man.

Billy passes the joint to Tim. Tim takes a long hard drag.

Tim   That's a rare joint.

Billy   Ye know – ma da used to get stoned when we went campin in Donegal.

Tim   Campin in Donegal – I should've clocked on then you were a Tim.

Billy   An that is a great joint.

Tim   How d'ye know E.T.'s a Catholic?

Billy   Dunno?

Tim   Ye jist need to look at him.

Both laugh.

Billy   How d'ye know E.T's a Proddy?

Tim   Ye jist need to look at him?

Billy   He's no – he wouldn't associate wi us
        Orange bastards. (*they laugh*) Mon we'll
        sing a song.

Tim   Soldiers are we...

Billy   Not a bigoted wan. Jist a song.

Tim   Aw – right. (*They think about what song to
        sing*) What about – hey – what about –
        listen to this... (sings) I don't know if you
        can see... (*Billy hums some trying to
        remember it*) The changes that have come
        over me. (*Harry comes back*)

Billy   (*to Tim*) In these last few days I've been
        afraid.

Tim   (*to Billy*) That I might drift away...

Billy   (*to Tim*) So I've been telling old stories,

Tim   (*to Billy*) singing songs...

Billy   (*to Tim*) That make me think about where I
        came from.

Tim   (*to Billy*) And that's the reason why I seem...

B/T   So far away today (*they sing the song
        together with great gusto taking chances
        each at the joint, coughing spluttering and
        forgetting the words*)

Oh, but let me tell you that I love you
That I think about you all the time
Caledonia you're calling me
And now I'm going home
(*Harry comes up. He lifts the flask – looks for the cups*)
I have moved and I've kept on moving
Proved the points that I've needed proving
Lost the friends that I've needed losing
Found others on the way...

The door opens, Tim nips the joint and shoves it in the lavvy pan.

13

Tim   Jesus, Harry, ye frightened the fuckin pish out of us there, so ye did.

Harry's surprised to see them in different strips.

Harry   (*lifting flask cups*) Regained consciousness and everything's going to be alright.

Billy and Tim are visibly relieved.

Billy   Good news, Harry.

Tim   Aw that's great, so it is.

Billy   I bet ye're relieved.

Harry   A happier man you'll not see this side of the Luggie Burn.

Billy   We sayed a prayer.

Tim The two of us.

Harry Seen it on the CCTV. Thanks lads. What's the story with the tops?

Tim I like this one. I'm keepin it.

Billy Aye. Me an all. I'm a temporary Tim.

Tim An I'm an honorary Hun.

Harry Was that a good peace pipe?

Tim Eh?

Harry The joint.

Tim What fuckin joint?

Harry The one you flicked down the cludgie. Right – mon – out.

Tim Eh?

Harry Out.

Billy Ye're not gettin polis for a daft joint are ye, Harry!

Tim Just a joint!

Harry No. You're free to go.

Tim   But it was a draw!

Harry   Your fines've been paid.

Tim   No they've not.

Billy   Naw they've no.

Harry   They have, I'm afraid.

A puzzled beat, then:

Billy   It was a draw!

Tim   Who paid them?

Harry   Me.

Tim   You?

Billy   You paid oor fines?

Tim   The two of us?

Harry   I need to get up to the hospital. So...

Tim   Ya fuckin beauty!

Billy   We'll pay ye back, Harry. Nat right, Tim?

Tim   Double. Promise!

Harry   Hey – don't geez your shite! Come on. Your

possessions are upstairs. Get your shoes.

As Harry leads them away Tim and Billy sing.

B/T   Oh, but let me tell you that I love you
        That I think about you all the time
        Caledonia you're calling me
        And now I'm going home

Clang! The door closes.

Afterword

TWO HATE FILLED Old Firm fans are put into a prison cell and verbally lacerate each other while their teams assemble on the park. Under the microscope, Des Dillon plays out all their fears, paranoia, misconceptions and most significantly a loathing that has shaped their whole lives. *Singin I'm No A Billy He's A Tim* was a word of mouth sensation at the 2005 Edinburgh Fringe Festival; a last-minute addition to the programme, it proved to be a success with virtually no advertising and press. As a Catholic Celtic supporter from Coatbridge, Des was particularly keen to provide a sincere reflection of the social, theological, geographical and ethnic backgrounds of the two sets of supporters and their cultural identities. By his own admission, there has been more deliberation towards Rangers, leaving him able to reflect on the positives and negatives of the Old Firm with a clear conscience. Readers, however, shouldn't worry about what foot Des kicks with, in fact it's exactly that kind of attitude the play wants to challenge. If marketing gurus got their hands on Des, they would probably brand him 'The People's Writer'. Last year, the previous Writer in Residence at Castlemilk won a World Book Day award with *Me and My Gal* for its articulation of modern Scottish life. His play *Six Black Candles*, a contemporary tale of female ritualistic revenge set in Coatbridge, was premiered at the Royal Lyceum in Edinburgh. Although considered a major new influence in Scottish writing, his is a voice full of Irish linguistics blending with a modern-day Scottish ethos.

Singin I'm No A Billy He's A Tim accurately reflects both cultures, whilst taking a humorous and insightful look at the bigotry that exists in the west of Scotland. Dillon pulls the audience in with laughs but towards the end of play, Billy and Tim have an almost religious experience and unique understanding of the other side: for better or worse, they need, rely, function and live for each other. Already the Scottish Executive is making plans to stage the play in schools across the country. Des has also taken heart from both sets of supporters giving him positive feedback – something that has proved difficult, as no two fans of either club are the same. He told me: 'I'm not one for saying "we need to educate people" but both sets of fans need to know what the other is all about. If you come to see this play, it actually lets each other see what the other is really like. We're a pair of eejits – the two of us but the rivalry and the hatred has to drop a level. We need to get rid of the suspicion and the paranoia. I've gave the Celtic fan in this play all the paranoia but in reality both sets of supporters are paranoid.'

Initially the Rangers fan appears the most willing to admit his shortcomings; his role is certainly more compassionate and solicitous. Had it been the other way around, it's unlikely Des would be taken seriously, in light of his own background. 'I had to make the

Rangers fan the more lovable, to even up the balance. That was deliberate, because I'm a Catholic. I gave him characteristics that I might not normally have given him. I think it works that such a hard, closed-off guy suddenly comes out with these sentiments. It was astounding, and really just luck that it worked.' There is also some weighty dialogue challenging Old Firm views on ethnicity and lineage, perhaps one of the more dangerous and often contentious elements to the support. One of the major delusions he deals with early on is when Rangers fan Billy announces 'We took you in.' More significant is the suggestion that bigotry creates an alliance. 'It's no good without an enemy', admits Billy. Des doesn't take one side: here, the Celtic fan is embittered; he holds onto the mistakes of the past and is stunted by them. It's also a potent moment when staunch Orange Protestant Billy comes clean about his Irish Catholic roots. It's also a reflection on Des's world. 'He is a real character, based on my stepson. He was brought up a Rangers fan but genetically both his parents are Irish Catholic. He also has step grandparents who are as staunch Rangers as you can get, so I studied them for the play. Really that's where the whole idea came from. I started to support Rangers in Europe because of him; I find it really strange just now with Rangers playing Porto because there is a moment where Billy chants Porto in reference to the Seville game.' It's unusual to get supporters on the same side to agree let alone opposing members of the Old Firm but the kind of people who have a problem with this play are unreachable in the first instance. Says

Des: 'There is an element of right hard Celtic fans that are really embittered to the point that they've become spiritually crippled. This play is about human beings and if there's anyone on either side who has a problem with the play, then they are a bigot; if it storms up a hornet's nest, that's good.'

Paradoxically, a number of themes also unite both sets of supporters and how they are viewed by the rest of the world. He also takes an exigent look at the Catholic and Protestant influence, taking it out of a wanting culture and tuning it back into a more ethereal context. 'If you think about these two guys in a cell – they are empty inside and they are searching for something. They see a glimmer of something inside that cell. It's a big thing when the Rangers fan talks about society being anti-Christian. They both find a truth. There is no way I'm saying everything is going to be alright when they get out but they have the memory, they might look back and say something happened inside that cell – "that was weird; what was that?" That's the magic I try to conjure up in my writing; I always try to raise the stakes for the human race.'

Richard Purden

Richard Purden is a freelance writer from Edinburgh and has contributed to *Scotland on Sunday, The Herald, The Scotsman* and *The Irish Post*.

My Epileptic Lurcher
Des Dillon
ISBN 1 906307 22 9 HBK £12.99

That's when I saw them. The paw prints. Halfway along the ceiling they went. Evidence of a dog that could defy gravity.

The incredible story of Bailey, the dog who walked on the ceiling; and Manny, the guy who got kicked out of Alcoholics Anonymous for swearing.

Manny Riley is newly married, with a puppy and a wee flat by the sea, and the BBC are on the verge of greenlighting one of his projects. Everything sounds perfect. But Manny has always been an anger management casualty, and the idyllic village life is turning out to be more League of Gentlemen than The Good Life. The BBC have decided his script needs totally rewritten, the locals are conducting a campaign against his dog, and the village policeman is on the side of the neds. As his marriage suffers under the strain of his constant rages, a strange connection begins to emerge between Manny's temper and the health of his beloved Lurcher.

Laugh-out-loud funny, this brilliant novel breaks into a convincing Dogspeak that will ring true in any dog-loving household. Complete with all the jealousy and heartbreak that come into any loving relationship, dog-human relations have never been so vividly expressed. This is a book for anyone who has ever had a dog. Or talked to one.

... raw, immediate and affecting
THE BIG ISSUE

Monks
Des Dillon
ISBN 1 905222 75 0 PBK £7.99

Ye must've searched out solitude in your life. At least once.

Three men are off from Coatbridge to an idyllic Italian monastic retreat in search of inner peace and sanctuary.

... like hell they are. Italian food, sunshine and women – it's the perfect holiday in exchange for some east construction work at the monastery.

Some holiday it turns out to be, what with optional Mass at five in the morning, a mad monk with a ball and chain, and the salami fiasco – to say nothing of the language barrier.

But even on this remote and tranquil mountain, they can't hide from the chilling story of Jimmy Brogan. Suddenly the past explodes into the present, and they find more redemption than they ever bargained for.

They Scream When You Kill Them
Des Dillon
ISBN 1 905222 35 1 PBK £7.99

From pimps to Shakespeare, langoustines to lurchers, Dillon's short stories bite ... hard.

Welcome to Dillon's world; a world where murderous poultry and evolutionary elephants make their mark. Des takes you from the darkness of *The Illustrated Man* and *Jif Lemons* to the laugh out loud *Bunch of C*****.

These stories are instantly accessible and always personal. Relationships and places and language are set precisely with few words and no flinching. If you're an alcoholic, recovering alcoholic, insane, a policeman, prisoner, gold digger, farmer, animal lover, Scots Irish or Irish Scots you may well recognise yourself somewhere in this book.

A brilliant storyteller of his own people, of all people.
LESLEY RIDDOCH

The Glasgow Dragon
Des Dillon
ISBN 1 84282 056 7 PBK £9.99

What do I want? Let me see now. I want to destroy you spiritually, emotionally and mentally before I destroy you physically.

When Christie Devlin goes into business with a triad to take control of the Glasgow drug market little does he know that his downfall and the destruction of his family is being plotted. As Devlin struggles with his own demons the real fight is just beginning.

There are some things you should never forgive yourself for.

Will he unlock the memories of the past in time to understand what is happening?

Will he be able to save his daughter from the danger he has put her in?

Nothing is as simple as good and evil. Des Dillon is a master storyteller and this is a world he knows well.

Des Dillon writes like a man possessed. The words come tumbling out of him ... His prose ... teems with unceasing energy.
THE SCOTSMAN

Me and Ma Gal
Des Dillon
ISBN 1 84282 054 0 PBK £5.99

If you never had to get married an that I really think that me an Gal'd be pals for ever. That's not to say that we never fought. Man we had some great fights so we did.

A story of boyhood friendship and irrepressible vitality told with the speed of trains and the understanding of the awkwardness, significance and fragility of that time. This is a day in the life of two boys as told by one of them, 'Derruck Danyul Riley'.

Dillon captures the essence of childhood and evokes memories of long summers with your best friend. He explores the themes of lost innocence, fear and death; writing with subtlety and empathy through the character of Derruck.

Dillon's book is arguably one of the most frenetic and kinetic, living and breathing of all Scottish novels... The whole novel crackles with this verbal energy.
THE LIST 100 Best Scottish Books of All Time – 2005

Six Black Candles
Des Dillon
ISBN 1 906307 49 3 PBK £8.99

'Where's Stacie Gracie's head?' ... sharing space with the sweetcorn and two-for-one lemon meringue pies ... in the freezer.

Caroline's husband abandons her (bad move) for Stacie Gracie, his assistant at the meat counter, and incurs more wrath than he anticipated. Caroline, her five sisters, mother and granny, all with a penchant for witchery, invoke the lethal spell of the Six Black Candles.

Set in present day Irish Catholic Coatbridge, *Six Black Candles* is bound together by the ropes of traditional storytelling and the strength of female familial relationships. Bubbling under the cauldron of superstition, witchcraft and religion is the heat of revenge; and the love and venom of sisterhood.

A great dramatic situation, in which the primitive Darwinian passions of lust, rage, vengeance, and fierce family loyalty come into conflict with the everyday scepticism of the sisters' modern lives. Dillon spins physical and verbal comedy out of his scenario with all the flair of a born play-wright

THE SCOTSMAN

Picking Brambles
Des Dillon
ISBN 1 84282 021 4 PBK £6.99

The first pick from over 1,000 poems written by Des Dillon

I always considered myself to be first and foremost, a poet. Unfortunately nobody else did. The further away from poetry I moved the more successful I became as a writer. This collection for me is the pinnacle of my writing career. Simply because is my belief that poetry is at the cutting edge of language. Out there breaking new ground in the creation of meaning.

DES DILLON

Selected and introduced by Brian Whittingham.

...to spend an hour in Dillon's company and listen to his quick-fire verbal delivery is to sample the undiluted language of the man that is the raw-material used in the crafting of his writing. The computer terminology Dillon is a WYSIWYG person (What You See Is What You Get.) No airs and graces and no fancy lah-de-dahs, though in Dillon's case it's worth remembering, moving waters run deep.

BRIAN WHITTINGHAM

Help Me Rhonda
Alan Kelly
ISBN 1 905222 83 1 PBK £9.99

Rhonda. The answer's Rhonda. I hate Rhonda. Hate her with a passion. A desire. I love to hate her.

Sonny Jim McConaughy is no stranger to trouble. He blackmails his lawyer, scams the insurance company, drinks, takes drugs and sleeps around.

However, Sonny Jim has stumbled into more trouble than even he can handle, waking up to find himself accused of attempted murder with no memory of the previous drunken night. So his girlfriend Rhonda, determined to stop him destroying them both, pits herself against him in a desperate battle of attrition.

A book to make you laugh and cringe throughout, filled with grit, realism, dark humour and a hilarious cast of misfits.

…shares a flair for the colourful language and violent scenarios of the Trainspotting scribe.
THE EVENING TIMES

Eye for an Eye
Frank Muir
ISBN 1 905222 56 4 PBK £9.99

One psychopath. One killer. The Stabber.

Six victims. Six wife abusers. Each stabbed to death through their left eye.

The cobbled lanes and back streets of St Andrews provide the setting for these brutal killings. But six unsolved murders and mounting censure from the media force Detective Inspector Andy Gilchrist off the case. Driven by his fear of failure, desperate to redeem his career and reputation, Gilchrist vows to catch The Stabber alone.

What is the significance of the left eye? How does an old photograph of an injured cat link the past to the present? And what exactly is *our little group*? Digging deeper into the world of a psychopath, Gilchrist fears he is up against the worst kind of murderer – a serial killer on the verge of mental collapse.

Can Gilchrist unravel the crazed mind of the killer? With reckless resolve, he risks it all in a heartstopping race to catch The Stabber, knowing that any mistake could be his last.

Everything I look for in a crime novel.
LOUISE WELSH

Luath Press Limited
committed to publishing well written books worth reading

LUATH PRESS takes its name from Robert Burns, whose little collie Luath (*Gael.*, swift or nimble) tripped up Jean Armour at a wedding and gave him the chance to speak to the woman who was to be his wife and the abiding love of his life. Burns called one of 'The Twa Dogs' Luath after Cuchullin's hunting dog in Ossian's *Fingal*. Luath Press was established in 1981 in the heart of Burns country, and now resides a few steps up the road from Burns' first lodgings on Edinburgh's Royal Mile.

Luath offers you distinctive writing with a hint of unexpected pleasures.

Most bookshops in the UK, the US, Canada, Australia, New Zealand and parts of Europe either carry our books in stock or can order them for you. To order direct from us, please send a £sterling cheque, postal order, international money order or your credit card details (number, address of cardholder and expiry date) to us at the address below. Please add post and packing as follows: UK – £1.00 per delivery address; overseas surface mail – £2.50 per delivery address; overseas airmail – £3.50 for the first book to each delivery address, plus £1.00 for each additional book by airmail to the same address. If your order is a gift, we will happily enclose your card or message at no extra charge.

Luath Press Limited
543/2 Castlehill
The Royal Mile
Edinburgh EH1 2ND
Scotland

Telephone: 0131 225 4326 (24 hours)
Fax: 0131 225 4324
email: sales@luath.co.uk
Website: www.luath.co.uk